IN STITCHES WITH MS WIZ

Terence Blacker has been a full-time writer since 1983. In addition to the best-selling *Ms Wiz* stories, he has written a number of books for children, including *Pride and Penalties* and *Shooting Star* from the *Hotshots* series, *The Great Denture Venture*, *Nice Neighbours/Nasty Neighbours* and *Homebird*. *Ms Wiz Spells Trouble*, the first book in the *Ms Wiz* series, was shortlisted for the Children's Book Award 1988 and selected for the Children's Book of the Year 1989.

What the reviewers have said about *Ms Wiz*:

'Every time I pick up a Ms Wiz, I'm totally spellbound . . . a wonderfully funny and exciting read.' *Books for Keeps*

'Hilarious and hysterical.' Susan Hill, *Sunday Times*

'Terence Blacker has created a splendid character in the magical Ms Wiz. Enormous fun.' *The Scotsman*

'Sparkling zany humour . . . brilliantly funny.' *Children's Books of the Year*

Titles in the Ms Wiz series

Terence Blacker

IN STITCHES
WITH MS WIZ

Illustrated by Tony Ross

MACMILLAN
CHILDREN'S BOOKS

First published 1989 by Piccadilly Press Ltd
Young Piper edition published 1990 by Pan Books Ltd

This edition published 1996 by
Macmillan Children's Books
a division of Macmillan Publishers Limited
25 Eccleston Place, London SW1W 9NF
and Basingstoke

Associated companies throughout the world

ISBN 0 330 34764 0

1 3 5 7 9 8 6 4 2

A CIP catalogue record for this book is available from
the British Library.

Phototypeset by Intype London Ltd
Printed by Mackays of Chatham plc, Kent

For Xan

CHAPTER ONE

A Pain on Thursday

Have you ever seen an ambulance racing at top speed through the streets, overtaking cars, driving through red traffic lights, its siren blaring and its blue light flashing? Have you ever thought that it would be exciting to be riding in the back, behind the darkened windows of the ambulance?

Well, it isn't.

Jack Beddows loved going fast – he had always thought that he would like to be a fireman or policeman one day so that he could break the speed limit whenever he felt like it – but right now, as he lay in the back of an ambulance travelling at sixty miles an hour down a busy street, he

wasn't interested. In fact, he would have given anything to be back at home, lying in his bed, without this terrible pain in his stomach.

It was the worst stomach ache of all time and it had been getting more painful all day. It was so bad that he hadn't been able to concentrate at school. In the middle of the maths lesson, he had even started crying.

"Please, sir." Jack's friend Caroline had put up her hand. "Jack's feeling ill."

The new teacher, Mr Bailey, had continued writing on the blackboard. "I'm not surprised," he had said. "I felt ill when I looked at his work this morning."

"But sir—" Caroline had protested.

"Nice try, Jack," said Mr Bailey. "Just in time for the maths test on Monday. Very convenient, I must say."

The ambulance took a corner with a screech of tyres. Jack groaned.

If only Ms Wiz had still been at school, he thought. She had been the class teacher last term and, whenever there were problems, she somehow made it better with her magic spells. There was certainly nothing magic about Mr Bailey.

When Jack hobbled home after school, he had found his father messing around with the car, as usual.

"Dad," Jack had said to the pair of legs sticking out from under the car. "I've got a pain in my stomach."

His father continued working. "Have you been?" he asked eventually.

That was the sum total of his father's medical knowledge. Even when his little sister Jenny had complained of having toothache, it had been the same old question. Have you been?

By the time his mother had come back from the library where she worked, Jack had been sick twice.

"Down in the dumps?" she had asked cheerfully. "A bit under the weather?"

"No. Ill."

"Why not go and skateboard outside?"

"I'm too ill to skateboard."

"Ring the doctor, Dad," said Mrs Beddows. "I think it's serious."

It certainly felt serious, Jack thought as the ambulance finally came to a halt. The doors swung open. Jack was put on a trolley and wheeled into the hospital.

The nurse in the main hall looked

5

down at Jack. "How are we?" she asked.

Jack smiled weakly. "We're not very well," he said.

"Children's ward," said the nurse to the man pushing Jack's trolley. "The doctor will be right along. I'll get them to prepare the theatre."

Theatre? thought Jack as he was wheeled into a brightly-coloured ward. Here I am, dying, and they're

talking about the theatre. Weird.

The other children in the ward stared as a nurse drew the curtains around Jack's bed.

"Just slip out of your clothes," she said, "and pop into this."

She gave Jack what looked like a nightie.

"I'm a boy," he protested feebly.

"And this is a gown," said the nurse. "Hurry up. The Consultant

will be here in a minute."

Jack had just put on his gown when a tall man with a white coat poked his head around the curtains. The Consultant stood by Jack's bed and looked down at him like a vulture considering its breakfast. Behind him stood another doctor. She had her dark hair in a bun and wore rather peculiar glasses. Something about the way she smiled at him reminded Jack of someone he knew.

"Let's have a quick look at you," said the Consultant, pressing the right side of Jack's stomach with his cold hands.

"Ow," said Jack.

"Mm. Uncomfortable?"

"Yes," said Jack.

The Consultant turned to the nurse.

"Are the parents here?" he asked.

"They've been delayed," she said. "Apparently they were trying to follow the ambulance and had a small disagreement with a double-decker bus. They're all right. They rang to give their permission to operate."

Jack groaned. His first time in hospital and his father had driven into a bus while chasing the ambulance. Typical.

"We're going to give you a little operation," the Consultant said to Jack, as if it were some kind of treat. "We need to take out your appendix to make you feel better."

"What's an appendix?"

"It's a small, completely useless piece of gristle in your intestine," said the Consultant. "I promise you won't miss it. Now we'd better hurry because that naughty appendix really ought to come out soon."

That's just great, thought Jack, as he was wheeled off once again. I'm about to be cut open by someone who talks about a naughty appendix.

There was something else bothering him. It was the other doctor. Now where had he seen her before? He wished she were doing the operation. A lot of people smiled at the hospital but she was different – she looked as if she meant it.

"Mr Jones here is what we call the anaesthetist," said the Consultant when Jack arrived in another room. "He's going to give you a little prick in the arm and you'll fall asleep."

Was Jack dreaming already? The woman doctor had seemed to give him an enormous wink, as if they were old friends. As the anaesthetist bent over his arm, there was a familiar humming noise. The needle of the injection suddenly bent over, like a wilting flower.

It couldn't be, could it? Jack looked at her more closely. The hair was

different and she never used to have
glasses, but there was something
about the black nail varnish she was
wearing. Now where had he seen
black nail varnish?

"Funny," said the anaesthetist,
reaching for another needle.

"A lot of funny things are
happening in this hospital at the
moment," said the Consultant.
"Aren't they, Doctor Wisdom?"

Doctor Wisdom! It must be! She

had promised she'd see him again. What were her exact words? "I go wherever magic is needed." He certainly needed magic now.

Jack felt the injection go into his arm. He heard a voice saying, "Now just count to three."

"Hi, Ms . . . Wiiiii . . ."

And Jack was fast asleep.

CHAPTER TWO

Magic on Friday

Hospitalized!

The word spread like wildfire through St Barnabas School the day after Jack was taken into hospital. The Morris twins, who knew the family that lived next door to him, said he would be away from school for days. By break time, the rumour was that he would miss the rest of term. By lunch, it was generally agreed that Jack was unlikely ever to be seen at school again.

"What's 'hospitalized', sir?" Caroline asked Mr Bailey during Class Three's first lesson.

"It means that someone has to go into hospital," said the teacher, with a sympathetic smile. "Why, Caroline? Is it someone in your family?"

"It's Jack, sir. You remember that pain he had, sir – in maths?"

"Jack?" Mr Bailey looked worried. "I can't remember any pain."

"Siiir!" There were protests of disbelief from around the classroom.

"Yes, yes, all right. I remember now."

"Well, it got worse and worse," said

Caroline, who was beginning to enjoy herself now. "By the end of the day, he was *screaming* in agony."

"Don't be ridiculous, Caroline," said Mr Bailey nervously. "Er . . . really?"

"Hospitalized," said Caroline dramatically. She stared at Jack's empty seat. "Apparently the doctors only had one question. '*Why wasn't this child brought to us sooner?*' There's

going to be an investigation."

Mr Bailey had turned very pale.

"Um. Just got to visit the head teacher," he said, scurrying to the door with an anxious, hunted look. "Revise for your maths test, everyone. I'll be back in a minute."

The first time Jack woke up after his operation, he felt dizzy and sick. There was a tube sticking into his arm, he had a pain in his side, and his parents were talking at him.

Thinking that he almost preferred the stomach ache, he drifted off to sleep.

The second time Jack woke up after his operation, it was evening and his parents had gone home, but Ms Wiz was standing beside his bed.

"Ms Wiz!" Jack said weakly.

"Dr Wisdom at your service. I

thought you might be needing some special magic."

"Can you make me feel better?"

"I can't do that," said Ms Wiz, drawing the curtains around Jack's bed, "but I might be able to cheer you up a bit."

She reached into an inside pocket of her white coat and pulled out a china cat.

"Here's Hecate to look after you," she said, putting the cat on the bedside table. "Any time you need me, just tap her on the head."

"Thanks," croaked Jack.

"And you'll be needing some company," said Ms Wiz, putting her hand into another pocket and pulling out her tame, magic rat. "So Herbert will be staying with you until you're better."

She put Herbert the rat on to the bed. He sniffed around a bit and was

17

about to scurry under the bedclothes when Ms Wiz said, "Not there, Herbert – it's unhygienic. Under the pillow."

"But—" Jack tried to concentrate. "How did you get here?"

"They were expecting a supply doctor, whom I happened to know was ill. So I just turned up. They're so desperate for doctors here that they never even asked to see my papers."

"Cool," said Jack.

"Now, remember," said Ms Wiz, tucking up the bed. "Don't tell any of the nurses or doctors about our secret. They may not like the idea of magic spells in a modern hospital. They might even think I'm a sort of witch."

"Can I tell the other children?"

Ms Wiz looked around the ward and smiled.

"Of course you can," she said.

*

"She's never a witch."

The boy in the bed next to Jack's was called Franklyn. He had a bad back and he didn't believe in magic.

"Witches are for wimps," he said.

There was a hiss from Hecate, the china cat, and her eyes lit up.

"Nice toy," said Franklyn, unimpressed. He picked up his football magazine and started leafing through it.

Jack was too tired to argue.

"Just you wait and see," he said.

The next morning, the children's ward was visited by the Consultant. There was a group of medical students with him.

"I took this young man's appendix out yesterday," said the Consultant, when he reached Jack's bed. He turned to Ms Wiz, who was standing

at the back of the group. "How is he,
Dr Wisdom?"

"He's recovering well," said Ms
Wiz, with a little smile in Jack's
direction.

The Consultant turned to the
students and took a small bottle from
his pocket.

"And here," he said, "is the
appendix in question. As you can see
it was badly inflamed."

The students looked at the bottle

which seemed to contain a small red caterpillar, floating in liquid. The Consultant put the bottle down on the table beside Jack's bed.

"Let's have a look at the patient," he said. "Miss Harris, would you like to check his heart?"

One of the students stepped forward, put a stethoscope to her ears and placed the other end on Jack's heart. There was a faint humming noise from the direction of Ms Wiz. The student looked puzzled.

"Well?" said the Consultant. "What do you hear?"

"It seems to be disco music," said the student.

Jack winked at Franklyn who was now unable to hide his curiosity.

"Give me that stethoscope," said the Consultant. He listened to Jack's heart. "Extraordinary," he said.

"Excuse me," said Franklyn from the next bed. "There's a . . ."

But the Consultant was too busy looking at the stethoscope in his hand to pay any attention.

Jack now saw what Franklyn was staring at. Herbert the rat had escaped from under his pillow and, using the bedspread as cover, had made his way down to the foot of the bed. As the Consultant and his students examined the stethoscope, he

23

peeped out, ran to where the little bottle containing Jack's appendix stood, picked it up in his mouth and scurried back under the bedclothes.

"Excuse me—" said Franklyn again.

Jack put a finger to his lips and shook his head slowly.

"Yes, Franklyn?" asked Ms Wiz innocently. "Is something the matter?"

"Er, maybe not," said Franklyn.

CHAPTER THREE

A Visit on Saturday

It was Saturday morning, Jack's third day without an appendix, and Caroline and Podge had been allowed by their parents to walk to the hospital to visit him.

"How you feeling, Jacko?" asked Podge.

"Not bad," said Jack. "Considering I've had a major operation."

"Major operation," sniffed Franklyn from the next bed. "All they did was take out a small, completely useless piece of gristle."

"Oh no!" Caroline looked shocked. "You mean it was a brain operation?"

Jack started to laugh, then clutched his stomach. "Don't," he said. "It hurts when I laugh."

"I've got to admit that he's an interesting neighbour," Franklyn went on. "He thinks his doctor is a witch."

Podge looked amazed. "It's not . . .?"

"It is," smiled Jack.

"*And* he's got a rat under his pillow," Franklyn continued loudly.

"Sshh!" said Jack. "Don't let anyone know or there'll be trouble."

"Ah," said Franklyn. "Problem. I

think I just did – about five minutes ago."

At that moment, there was a scream from the other end of the ward.

News travels fast in a hospital. Franklyn had told his other neighbour Katie, who was suffering from asthma. Katie had told Matthew, who was hanging upside down with two broken legs. Matthew

had told Michelle, who was having tests. Michelle had told Amber, who had just had her tonsils out. Amber had whispered it to Tom, who had grommets. Tom had told his mother – and that was the scream from the other end of the ward.

"Now children," said the Ward Sister, as Tom's mother recovered on a spare bed. "You may have heard that a small, furry animal has been seen in here . . ."

"She means a rat," said Franklyn. There was a moan from Tom's mother.

". . . and small, furry animals are not welcome in hospitals, even if they are pets. So the nurses are going to search the ward."

"What will you do if you find it?" asked Jack.

"Confiscate it, of course," said the Ward Sister. "We're lucky enough to have an experimental laboratory downstairs. They always need fresh mice and rats."

Caroline and Podge gasped. Jack calmly leant over and tapped Hecate the cat's head. Her eyes flashed.

"Morning, Sister," said Ms Wiz, who breezed into the ward within seconds.

"Morning, Dr Wisdom."

Ms Wiz glanced at the nurses as they looked under the beds and in cupboards.

"Goodness," she said. "What's going on here?"

The Ward Sister whispered something in her ear.

"A *rat*?" Ms Wiz seemed shocked. "In that case, I'll just check the Beddows boy's dressing and leave you to it."

Ms Wiz hurried over to Jack's bed and pulled the curtains around it.

"Up to your old tricks, eh Ms Wiz?" said Caroline quietly.

"Just trying to cheer Jack up," said Ms Wiz, feeling under his pillow, eventually pulling out Herbert.

"Have you got one of those cardboard bottle things?" she asked Jack.

"You don't mean—?"

"That's right. The little bottles they give you to pee in when you're in bed."

Jack passed it to Ms Wiz, who had just slipped Herbert into the bottle when the curtains drew back. It was the Ward Sister.

"Jack's been a good boy, has he?" she said, looking at the bottle in Ms Wiz's hands.

"Er, yes."

"Allow me, Doctor," said the Ward Sister, taking the bottle. "I'll just get rid of this for you."

She was halfway across the ward when Herbert decided to put his head out for a quick look around. The Ward Sister shrieked and dropped the bottle.

"What on earth is going on?" The Consultant, who had heard the noise while passing, stood at the door. With a shaky hand, the Ward Sister pointed to Herbert who was coolly looking up at them.

"Stand back, everyone," shouted the Consultant, grabbing a long brush that was leaning against the wall. "Look away if you don't like the sight of squashed rodent."

He raised the brush over his head.

There was a humming noise from the direction of Ms Wiz.

Suddenly, the brush seemed to develop a life of its own. It leapt out of the Consultant's hands and pushed

him towards an empty corner bed. As he fell back, the curtains drew around the bed. There were sounds of scuffling.

Not looking particularly alarmed, Herbert sidled down one side of the room and out of the door.

Ms Wiz held up her hands.

"Keep calm," she said. "The rat has left the room. I'm sure he'll turn up—" for a moment she looked worried "—um, somewhere."

"Did you see that brush, Doctor?" gasped the Ward Sister.

"I'm sure there's a perfectly logical explanation for that," said Ms Wiz, walking towards the door.

There were muffled sounds of protest from the corner bed.

"What about the Consultant?" asked the Ward Sister.

Ms Wiz drew back the curtains. The Consultant was swathed head to foot in bandages. He looked like an Egyptian mummy.

"Let me out!" he gasped. "Someone's going to pay for this!"

"Wow," said Franklyn, as the Consultant was wheeled out of the ward to have his bandages removed. "Your Ms Wiz is the strangest doctor I've ever seen."

"If it wasn't for you, Herbert wouldn't be wandering around the hospital," said Caroline.

"He'll be all right," said Jack. "After all, he's a magic rat."

Franklyn pulled the bedclothes up to his chin. "I'm not letting that Ms Wiz anywhere near me," he said. "She may be a good witch but I don't trust her as a doctor."

Caroline looked at her watch. "We'd better go, Podge," she said.

"Remember we've got to revise for the maths test."

"Wait a minute," he said. "I want to ask Jack a few more questions."

Jack sighed.

"This pain you had," said Podge. "Which side was it on?"

Podge appeared to be deep in thought. He had just had a rather brilliant idea.

CHAPTER FOUR

Lunch on Sunday

Mr Bailey was a worried man.

It was only his second year as a teacher and he was finding it very difficult. The children didn't seem to respect him somehow. Whatever he asked them to do, they did the opposite. They laughed at him behind his back. And they were always playing tricks on him.

That was what happened with Jack Beddows. He had been certain that Jack's stomach ache was just another trick. There was a big maths test on Monday and Jack hated maths.

But it wasn't. The stomach ache was real. Jack was in hospital and Mr Bailey was in trouble.

Mr Gilbert, the head teacher at St

Barnabas, had not been pleased when
he heard what had happened.

"I take a dim view, Mr Bailey," he
had said. "After all, children are
people, you know."

"Are they?" Mr Bailey had said. He
wasn't sure any more.

"Why not," the head teacher had
sounded tired, "try to be nice for a
change?"

"Yes, Mr Gilbert."

Which was why, this Sunday

morning, Mr Bailey was going to visit the hospital. He had bought some flowers and a bunch of grapes and a Get Well card.

Maybe if he was nice to Jack, Class Three would be nice to him. It was worth a try.

Ms Wiz was worried too.

Ever since the Consultant had been pushed around by a brush and wrapped up like a Christmas present, he had been giving her very suspicious looks.

"It's strange," he said, as they did their morning rounds of the wards. "You turn up at the hospital as if by magic, and since then nothing's been quite normal. Bending needles, musical stethoscopes, flying brushes, rats. Where is that animal by the way?"

Ms Wiz shook her head. She hadn't the faintest idea where Herbert was. Secretly, she was afraid that he might decide to investigate the experimental laboratory. He could be quite a mischievous little rat sometimes.

"Yes, it is rather strange," she said.

"What's more, you're never around when real medical work is needed."

Ms Wiz laughed. "Perhaps that's a good thing," she said.

"Morning, nurse," said Jack's father to the Ward Sister as he arrived for his morning visit. "Has he been yet?"

"Dad!" protested Jack.

"Not yet," smiled the Ward Sister. "It takes a while after an appendix operation. Once he moves his bowels, we'll know he's really on the mend."

"What are bowels?" asked Jack's little sister Jenny.

"Things inside you that move from time to time," said Mrs Beddows.

"Not very often in Jack's case," boomed his father.

Jack noticed a familiar figure standing at the ward door, looking confused. At last, Mr Bailey spotted him.

"Hullo, young lad," he said. "I've brought you some goodies."

"Thank you," said Jack. "These are my parents and my sister. This is Mr Bailey."

The smile left the teacher's face.

"It . . . it wasn't my fault," he stammered. "They're always saying they've got stomach aches. Or ear aches. Or they feel sick. Particularly when there's a maths test coming up. You don't know who to believe, do you? They're such liars, children. I mean, not Jack – but the others . . . I didn't know it was an appendix. I'm not a doctor, am I? You can't blame me for that . . . can you?"

"Don't worry, Mr Bailey," said Jack's mother. "We all make mistakes."

There was an embarrassed silence.

"So," Jack said eventually. "Who'd like to see my appendix?"

*

It was a tiring morning for Jack. Mr Bailey always had that effect on him and watching him trying to impress his parents somehow made it even worse. So, when a nurse brought him lunch on a tray, he didn't feel the slightest bit hungry.

"Come on, Jack," said his mother. "You'll never get well if you don't eat."

"I just don't feel up to plastic chicken and stringy red cabbage," said Jack.

"Yum," said Mr Bailey loudly. "It looks delicious to me."

Quite why Ms Wiz walked into the ward at this particular moment, Jack never discovered. She was pretending to look at Tom, the boy with grommets, but Jack could tell that she was up to something from the quiet humming noise that was coming from her direction.

The bottle containing his appendix was on a table behind where Mr Bailey and his parents were sitting. This meant that only Jack and Franklyn saw the bottle open quietly. As if it were a real, live caterpillar, the appendix wriggled out.

"Just eat a bit," Jack's father was saying. "A mouthful for each of us."

The appendix crawled along the edge of the table.

"It's getting cold," said his sister.

Jack was speechless. The appendix was making its way on to the lunch tray – and into the red cabbage.

"I know what we'll do," said Mr Bailey. "I'll eat a mouthful, then you eat a mouthful."

"I don't think—"

"Here's a spare spoon," interrupted Franklyn, with an innocent little smile.

"Er, Mr Bailey—" said Jack.

But it was too late. The teacher dipped his spoon into the red cabbage. Jack closed his eyes. When he opened them, Mr Bailey was chewing with a slightly pained smile. The appendix had gone.

"Delicious," said Mr Bailey, swallowing with some difficulty.

Jack glanced over to where Ms Wiz was standing. He really thought she had gone too far this time. She shrugged helplessly.

"That's odd," said Franklyn, pointing at the empty appendix bottle. "Your spare part's gone missing."

"So it has," said Jack.

"Funny how similar to red cabbage it looks," said Franklyn.

Mr Bailey looked at the empty bottle and then at the half-eaten plate of cabbage. Suddenly he felt a little queasy.

"Better be going now," he said, getting unsteadily to his feet.

"Bye, sir," said Jack. "Thanks for coming."

Mr Bailey walked quickly out of the hospital towards his car. It couldn't have been, could it? That red cabbage *had* tasted a little rubbery.

Perhaps the story would get out. Jack would be bound to spread it around. It would probably get into the local paper. He could see the headlines now. "CRUEL TEACHER EATS BOY'S APPENDIX."

"Why me?" he shouted to an empty car park. He kicked his car, hurting his foot. "Why is it always me?"

CHAPTER FIVE

Mayhem on Monday

Ms Wiz had looked everywhere for Herbert. She had visited all the wards in the hospital. She had checked in the reception hall. She had even searched the kitchen. The only place where she had yet to look was the experimental laboratory, which had been locked up over the weekend.

Now it was Monday morning and Ms Wiz was on her way to the laboratory. It was her last chance. After all, life wouldn't be the same without Herbert.

"Dr Wisdom!"

Ms Wiz heard a familiar voice behind her as she hurried down a corridor. She turned to see the Consultant.

"Where are you going?" he asked.

"I was just looking in on the
laboratory," said Ms Wiz. "Er, I'm
rather interested in an experiment
they're doing."

"You're looking for that rat, aren't
you?"

"Rat?"

"You know what I think?" The
Consultant put his face close to hers. "I
don't think you're a doctor at all. I've
seen the way you go pale at the sight

of blood. You're never around when I need help with an operation. I think you're an intruder."

Ms Wiz smiled. She was wondering whether she should turn him into a rabbit. Perhaps not, she decided. A rabbit hopping about the hospital with a stethoscope around its neck would make people even more suspicious.

"I'm going to check your papers," said the Consultant. "If it turns out you're not a real doctor, I'm calling the police. Impersonating a doctor – that's serious." He smiled coldly. "They'll probably send you to prison."

Jack was sitting on the edge of his bed. Although his stomach was still sore and he was a bit weak, he was feeling much better. His parents were going to take him home that morning.

"So it's goodbye again," said Ms
Wiz, who was doing her normal round
of the children's ward. "Your stitches
will come out in a few days' time and
you'll be as good as new."

"Thank you for looking after me,"
said Jack. "Having an appendix out
isn't so bad after all."

"I think you should go and see Mr
Bailey as soon as you can," said Ms
Wiz. "After all, he visited you."

"Do us some more tricks, Doc,"
said Franklyn. "I'm going out
tomorrow and I'll have something
to tell them."

"No more tricks, I'm afraid,
Franklyn. I'm leaving today."

"What about Herbert?" asked Jack.

"He'll just have to look after
himself," said Ms Wiz. "I can't find
him anywhere."

Just then, the doors of the ward
opened and the Consultant strode in,

his white coat flapping. There were two policemen with him.

"That's her!" he said, pointing at Ms Wiz. "She's the imposter."

"But that's Dr Wisdom," said the Ward Sister.

"Doctor? Hah!" The Consultant's voice echoed round the children's ward as the two policemen advanced towards Ms Wiz.

One of them, who had now produced a notebook, asked, "Are you Doctor, or Miss Dolores Wis—?"

At that moment, the swing doors behind the Consultant crashed open and a white tidal wave of live, squeaking creatures poured into the ward.

"What on earth—?" gasped the Consultant.

Mice! Hundreds of them, swarming around the floor, climbing the curtains, exploring every corner. And, in the thick of them, standing up on his hind legs and looking about him, like a general surveying the field of battle, was Herbert.

"There you are, Herbert," said Ms Wiz, reaching down for him. "So you were in the laboratory, after all, were you? Freeing all the mice."

Jack picked his way through the swarm of white mice and whispered something in the Consultant's ear.

"Dr Wisdom," the Consultant shouted over the din. "Rid the hospital of these creatures and you can go free – I'll drop all charges against you."

Ms Wiz raised her hand and whistled. The mice froze, staring at her with little pink eyes. She picked up Herbert and looked around the ward for the last time.

"Thanks, Jack," she said cheerfully. "See you again soon."

"And me, Ms Wiz," said Franklyn.

"Of course. Whenever a bit of magic's needed. Bye everyone." She waved to the other children before making her way out of the ward, followed by Herbert's mouse army.

"And so Ms Wiz saved the hospital from a plague of white mice," Jack told Class Three that afternoon when he visited them. Even Mr Bailey, who had allowed Jack to speak about hospital during a lesson, looking impressed.

"What will she do with the mice?" asked Caroline.

"Probably lead them to the countryside and set them free," said Jack.

Alex put his hand up. "Can we see your appendix?" he asked. "Caroline said you'd kept it in a bottle."

"Right, back to work, class," Mr Bailey interrupted nervously.

"Oh, I threw it away," said Jack. "Who wants an old piece of gristle anyway?"

He glanced at Mr Bailey, who smiled with relief. Perhaps the head teacher had been right. Children were humans, after all.

"By the way," asked Jack. "Where's Podge?"

An ambulance raced through the streets of the town, its siren blaring and its blue light flashing.

In the back lay the patient, moaning quietly and clutching his right side.

"It worked!" thought Podge, as the ambulance screeched around a corner. He had remembered everything Jack had told him about the appendix, Mr

Bailey had called the doctor, and here
he was on the way to hospital. All he
would have now was a small
operation, five days in hospital with
Ms Wiz looking after him, a few
stitches and that would be that. It
was a small price to pay for missing
the maths test.

The ambulance stopped. The doors
were opened and Podge was wheeled
on a stretcher towards the hospital.

"Hullo, Podge." It was Ms Wiz, with

Hecate under her arm. "What's up?"

"Appendix, Ms Wiz," groaned Podge.

Hecate's eyes lit up.

"Oh dear. What a pity I'm just going," said Ms Wiz. "In fact, I only came back to collect Hecate."

"Going?"

"So you'll just have to face your major operation all on your own."

Podge gulped. "Er, maybe . . ."

Ms Wiz laughed. "Lend us your stretcher, Podge," she said.

Podge thought for a moment, and then rolled off the stretcher.

"Oh well," he said. "It was worth a try."

"Thanks, Podge," said Ms Wiz, climbing on. The stretcher rose and hovered over the heads of the ambulance men.

"I'll be back – when you're least expecting me," she called out as the

stretcher rose higher, turned slowly
and floated over the roof of the
hospital and out of sight.

As Podge and the ambulance men
watched Ms Wiz disappear, a nurse
walked out of the hospital. She had a
clipboard under her arm.

"Well, young man," she said. "Let's
get you registered. How's the pain
now?"

"Better, thank you," said Podge.
"Suddenly much better."